This book belongs to

____

SHERLOCK HOUND
AND THE CASE OF THE MYSTERIOUS MISSING PUMPKIN

Illustrated By
Scott Ross

From The Case Files Of
Dr. Bulldog Watson

The Unicorn Publishing House, Inc.
Morris Plains, New Jersey

Sherlock Hound

From his Baker Street flat, Sherlock Hound looked down upon the busy, bustling streets of London town. He heaved a heavy sigh, and then returned to his desk. For most of the morning, the great detective had busied himself in the practical study of pawprints, a useful skill for any sleuth.

"You seem troubled this morning, Sherlock," his good friend, Dr. Watson, remarked.

"Do I, Watson? Well, perhaps I am," answered Sherlock Hound. Then after a moment, he said, "Or better to say I am restless, Watson, restless! I take the greatest pleasure in my books, my studies, my experiments, but it is the chase I love, Watson, the chase!" And Watson could see Sherlock Hound's face brighten with just the thought of it. "There are villains afoot, Watson, and I want to catch them! The rascals and rogues of London shall not escape me!"

At that moment, a knock came at the door.

"Ah-ha, Watson! I smell a case brewing here. Please, by all means, let our mysterious guest in."

Dr. Watson went to the door. There at the entrance was the most beautiful, and by all accounts, the most wealthy feline in all of London, Madame La Chatte.

"By my word, come—come in, dear lady," stammered Dr. Watson, quite taken by the graceful beauty of their guest.

"My dear madame," began Sherlock; "what could possibly bring the toast of all London, her finest jewel, to my humble home?"

"Oh, Mr. Hound, I beg of you, help me. I am very nearly at my wits' end! Something—*something* must be done!"

"Madame, calm yourself," urged Dr. Watson. "Put your fears to rest, for in Sherlock Hound you have found a friend."

"Quite right, Watson," Sherlock said. "Now, please sit, and tell me everything, right from the beginning."

"The beginning—yes; well, that would have to be last night, when Old Tom brought us the pumpkin."

"A pumpkin?" Sherlock interrupted.

"Yes, and not just any pumpkin, but simply the most beautiful pumpkin I have ever seen," said Madame.

"I deduce, madame, that the pumpkin is to be the highlight of your annual Halloween Ball, is it not?"

"*Was*, Mr. Hound, was; for you see, someone has *stolen* it."

"By Jove, Sherlock!" Watson cried, "what foul business is this?"

"We shall soon see, Watson. Pray, continue, madame."

"Everything was splendid! I carved the face in the pumpkin myself. My great-aunt, the maid, the butler, and Old Tom, our gardener, all helped set a wonderful table for the party. We decorated the ballroom from top to bottom, and didn't finish till well past midnight. But when I came into the ballroom this morning, the pumpkin was gone!"

Madame La Chatte

HAPPY HALLOWEEN

"Except for those in the house that you have already mentioned, did anyone else pay you a visit last night?" Sherlock asked.

"No, Mr. Hound, no one," Madame La Chatte replied, "and all the doors and windows were locked down tight. I can't understand how someone could have gotten in. It is a complete mystery to me."

"Yes, a mystery indeed," echoed Sherlock.

"Can you help, Mr. Hound?" Madame pleaded. "The party is this very night, and there are simply no more pumpkins to be found in all of London. I have called in Scotland Yard, but they seem completely baffled by the case."

"Indeed," Sherlock said, raising one brow slightly. "Don't fear, madame, we will soon get to the bottom of this. Come, Watson," Sherlock cried, as he grabbed his pipe and magnifying glass. "Hurry now, for the *game* is afoot!"

And they were off in a flash for Madame's manor.

The Pumpkin

Upon arriving by coach at the manor, Sherlock Hound wasted no time in gathering up clues. "You're Tom, Madame's gardener?" Sherlock asked.

"Aye, sir, that I am," Old Tom replied, hobbling forward a couple of steps.

"Think now; when you brought the pumpkin home, did you see anyone who might be following you?"

"Nooooo, sir, that I didn't," Old Tom said, "but I—I felt something, I'm not quite sure I should say. . . ."

"What did you feel, Tom?" Sherlock pressed him. "Don't worry; be a good fellow now and tell us."

"Well, Mr. Hound, when I came into the house, I—I felt unseen eyes upon me. It was just as if the house itself had eyes!" Old Tom whispered, casting a fearful glance over his back toward the house.

"A house with *eyes*! Oh, really now, Sherlock, you don't . . ."

"We shall see, Watson, we shall see," Sherlock simply said.

Old Tom Cat

In the hallway of the manor, Sherlock ran into Scotland Yard's Chief Inspector and his lowly assistant.

"Mr. Sherlock Hound, is it now," the Chief Inspector said, frowning a bit. "I dare say even London's most, *uh-humph*, celebrated detective will be of little help here."

"Perhaps, Chief Inspector, you are right," Sherlock replied, politely; "but an extra pair of eyes and another sniffing snout can hardly hurt."

"Sniff away, Mr. Hound, sniff away," the Chief Inspector said; "but you'll find nothing here, I assure you. We have gone over this house from top to bottom. A mystery it is and a mystery it will remain."

"We will soon see if that is true, Inspector. Come, Watson; the answers we seek are not here, but at the scene of the crime." And Sherlock made straightaway for the ballroom.

CHIEF

The ballroom was just as Madame La Chatte had described it. Everything had been readied for the upcoming costume ball. Sherlock took out his magnifying glass and began looking for clues to the crime.

"What can I do to assist you, Sherlock?" Watson asked, as he looked longingly at some of the cakes and cookies already set out for the party.

"You, my good friend, should bring everyone in the house to this room. I will have need to question them."

Reluctantly, Watson left the goodies on the table, and set off to gather up the household. He soon returned with Madame, her Auntie, the maid, and the butler. Old Tom wouldn't come inside, claiming that the house was haunted.

"What is the meaning of this, Mr. Hound?" asked Auntie. "We have already told Scotland Yard all we know."

"I'm sure, dear lady," Sherlock said gently; "but I have need to hear all accounts of last night, that nothing might be missed."

"Well, I never!" huffed Auntie. "Oh, very well then, if it *must* be done." And all in turn gave their accounts of the previous night.

"What do you think happened, Mr. Hound?" Madame asked, when everyone had finished speaking.

"I do not yet know what happened, madame, but I do know what didn't happen."

"What's that, Sherlock?" Watson asked.

"That the pumpkin could not have been taken by anyone *outside* of this house."

"But surely, Mr. Hound, you're not accusing . . ." Madame began, but broke off, saying, "Oh, Derek, you have come!"

"Yes, dear lady, I came as soon as I heard," said Derek, taking Madame La Chatte's hand and patting it. "Simply, simply awful, I must say. If I could lay my hands on the villain that did this, believe you me, I would—"

"I think Mr. Hound here was about to accuse one of us," interrupted Madame. "Isn't that right, Mr. Hound?"

"My dear chap, you don't really believe . . ." Derek began.

"No, I don't," Sherlock answered. "I have simply made a logical deduction based on the facts so far. It is clear from your accounts that all the doors and windows were locked last night, including the door to the ballroom. This morning, the door and windows of the ballroom were still locked, but the pumpkin was gone. Therefore, I deduce that the thief came from within, not without."

"But if you don't believe any of them did it, *who* did?" asked Watson, quite confused.

"That is what you and I, Watson, are about to find out."

Derek, The Playboy

Sherlock climbed upon a large table, the table where the pumpkin had been placed, and began to look carefully through his magnifying glass. After a moment, Sherlock said to himself, half amused, "Yes, Old Tom must be right, the house does have eyes!"

"Eyes?!" exclaimed Watson. "Oh, really Sherlock, not that rubbish again. I mean, the poor fellow didn't know what he was saying."

"I have it, Watson!" Sherlock shouted, as he jumped from the table. "There is another way into this room than just the door and the windows. There is a *secret* entrance!"

"Are you sure, Sherlock, I mean . . ."

"Quick, Watson, search the walls and floor for a hidden door. We must act before they get wise to us and flee!"

Watson stood, looking about and saying to himself, "Secret entrance?! They?! Who *are* they?"

"Watson, there is no time! I will explain later. Quickly now!"

The Pumpkin

Sherlock Hound and his friend, Watson, carefully combed over the entire ballroom. They looked along the floor, the fireplace, the bookcase, but found nothing. Until . . .

"I say, Sherlock, I'm pooped!" Watson huffed, and he leaned against the fireplace. As he did so, one of the carvings on the mantel moved. "I'm sorry, old fellow, but I really don't think . . . Oooohhh, myyyy worrrd!" At that moment, a secret door opened, and Watson fell backward into a dark passage.

"Well done, Watson!" Sherlock laughed. "You have found it, old fellow, you have *found* it!"

The butler brought a lantern and lit it. Sherlock turned to Derek, saying, "Sir, you may now have your chance to get your hands on these villains. Perhaps you would care to lead our little party?"

"Who, me? I'd rather not . . . I mean, someone must stay and protect Madame, right? I leave this awful business in your capable, yes, most *capable* hands, sir." And Derek drew closer to Madame.

"Very well; come, Watson!" And the two disappeared down the dark passage.

"Sherlock, shouldn't we get the help of Scotland—"

"Shhhh, Watson! My nose tells me we are very close. Stay right behind me, and we will soon find—aha! There they are, Watson! Hold; hold, I say!"

"Oh, I say!" cried Watson. "Why, they are rats! My word!"

"Not precisely, Watson. Better to say they are Rat-Robbers."

"Rat-Robbers, Rat-Robbers, we rob you day and night,
Rat-Robbers, Rat-Robbers, don't we look a fright?
We creep, we crawl, through room and hall,
Stealing what we please.
A bit of cake or cookie paste,
Or, oh! a wedge of cheese!
We're Rat-Robbers, Rat-Robbers, we'll take a bite or two.
And if we please, you will see, we'll take a bite of—"

"Oh, really now, that is quite enough!" declared Watson.

"Quite," said Sherlock.

"Out with it now; the game's up!" Watson said. "There's no use in hiding anything. Where is Madame's pumpkin?"

"The answer, my nose tells me, lies in the room beyond, Watson," Sherlock said. And sure enough, in a large room nearby, the Rat-Robbers were busy making pumpkin pies!

"Oh dear, Sherlock, we have arrived too late!" Watson moaned. "Madame's party will be ruined!"

One Rat-Robber stepped forward. "Please, Mr. Hound, we meant no harm," he said.

"We meant no harm!" came a chorus from the Rat-Robbers. "Anyway, those cats have everything!" a voice called from the back. The others nodded in agreement: "*Yeah*!"

"Now see here; that may well be," scolded Watson; "but that gives you no right to go sneaking about in the dead of night like—like common criminals, rascals, rogues! stealing from such a fine feline as Madame La Chatte!"

"Well said, Watson," agreed Sherlock; "but if these Rats will promise . . ."

"We promise! We promise!" sang the Rats.

"As I was saying, if these Rats promise not to misbehave in the future, I think I know a way to save Madame's party."

"We will! *We will*!" they all cried.

Rat-Robbers

"Oh, thank you, Mr. Hound!" Madame La Chatte cried. "The costume party is a complete success! I must admit I had my doubts at first, but the guests simply adore your idea."

"I am happy I could be of service, madame," Sherlock said as he bowed to her.

"Who would have thought of it," Madame said; "instead of a carved pumpkin for Halloween—pumpkin pie! And served to the guests by masked Rat-Robbers, no less! Delightful, simply delightful!"

"By Jove, Sherlock, you've done it!" laughed Watson, as he grabbed his fifth slice of pie.

"Quite, Watson, quite," Sherlock simply said.

Madame La Chatte

HAPP
CHIEF

Back at the Baker Street flat, Sherlock Hound and Dr. Watson lounged comfortably by the fireplace, sipping a spot of tea and tasting of a few sweet cakes.

"Tell me, Sherlock, how *did* you know about the Rat-Robbers?" Watson asked between sips and munches.

"Elementary, my dear Watson," Sherlock replied. "I knew what had become of Madame's pumpkin before I reached the door. My nose, you see, could detect the faint smell of pumpkin pie. Not knowing where the smell came from, I looked for some trace of the thief on the table in the ballroom. Through my magnifying glass I discovered that tiny pawprints, or rather ratprints, were left after they had stepped in some spilled sugar. Knowing the door and windows to be locked, I deduced there must be another entrance—underground. And you, my dear friend, did the rest when you fell through the passageway."

"Bravo, Sherlock, bravo!"

"Thank you, Watson," Sherlock said, with a slight nod. "And that, Watson, puts an end to the case of the mysterious missing pumpkin."

The Pumpkin

For information, contact: Jean L. Scrocco,
Unicorn Publishing House, 120 American Road,
Morris Plains, NJ 07950
Printed In U.S.A.

Printing History 15 14 13 12 11 10 9 8 7 6 5 4 3 2 1

This book is dedicated to
Wendy Michele

The End